Louanne Pig in
Making the Team

Louanne Pig in Making the Team

Nancy Carlson

Carolrhoda Books, Inc. / Minneapolis

Carolrhoda Books, Inc.
A division of Lerner Publishing Group
241 First Avenue North
Minneapolis, MN 55401 U.S.A.

Website address: www.lernerbooks.com

Library of Congress Cataloging-in-Publication Data

Carlson, Nancy L.
	Louanne Pig in making the team / by Nancy L. Carlson.
		p. cm.
	Summary: Though she plans to try out for cheerleading, Louanne Pig helps her friend Arnie try out for football, with surprising results.
	ISBN-13: 978–1–57505–914–3 (lib. bdg. : alk. paper)
	ISBN-10: 1–57505–914–2 (lib. bdg. : alk. paper)
	[1. Sex role—Fiction. 2. Pigs—Fiction. 3. Football—Fiction.] I. Title: Making the team. II. Title.
PZ7.C21665Lj 2005
[E]—dc22

Manufactured in the United States of America
1 2 3 4 5 6 – JR – 10 09 08 07 06 05

This book is dedicated to the memory of my dog,
Dame—my best pal. I miss her.

One day Louanne and Arnie found something exciting on the school bulletin board. Tryouts for the cheerleading squad and the football team were coming up.

"I'm going to try out for cheerleading," said Louanne.

"And I'm going to try out for the football team," said Arnie.

That afternoon they hurried over to Arnie's
to practice together.

Louanne was doing pretty well . . .

until she came to the split jump. She couldn't get off the ground.

"Like this, Louanne," said Arnie.

"I'm better at cartwheels," said Louanne.

"Let me show you how to do it," said Arnie.

"You ought to be practicing football," said
Louanne, and she picked up the football and
threw it to Arnie.

Arnie missed the catch.

"You have to keep your eye on the ball, Arnie,"
Louanne told him. "Like this."

"I'm probably better at tackling," said Arnie.

"Let me show you how to do it," said Louanne.

"Let's try some kicking," said Arnie.

All week long, Louanne and Arnie met after
school to practice for their tryouts. Louanne's jumps
didn't improve much, but Arnie kept her spirits up.
"You really look great!" he told her.

Arnie only rarely caught the ball, but Louanne encouraged him.

"I know you're going to make the team!" she said.

When the big day arrived, their confidence was high.

Cheerleading tryouts were first.

Louanne didn't make the squad.

"Don't feel bad," Arnie consoled her. "There's always next year. By then you'll be top-notch."

"Right," said Louanne. "Come on. There's still a little time before your tryout. I'll show you a few last tricks."

Arnie didn't.

Suddenly Louanne had an idea.

"Come on, Arnie!" she said. "Cheerleading tryouts are still going on."

That fall Roosevelt School won every game.
Louanne led the team to victory,

and Arnie led the cheers.